ZOMBIE CAMP

Speeding Star
an imprint of
Enslow Publishers, Inc.

ZOMBIE ZAPPERS
by Nadia Higgins
Book 1

Library of Congress Cataloging-in-Publication Data

Higgins, Nadia.
  Zombie camp / Nadia Higgins.
     p. cm. — (Zombie Zappers ; bk. 1)
  Summary: "Get to know Zombie Zappers Leo, Chad, and the rest of the gang as they try to solve the mystery of the Smellerd zombies at summer camp. What nightmarish surprise will they find waiting for them at Lake Moan?"—Provided by publisher.
  ISBN 978-1-62285-003-7
  [1. Zombies—Fiction. 2. Camps—Fiction.] I. Title.
  PZ7.H5349558Zoc 2013
  [Fic]—dc23

                          2012028661

Future editions:
Paperback ISBN: 978-1-62285-000-6   EPUB ISBN: 978-1-62285-002-0
Single-User PDF ISBN: 978-1-62285-004-4   Multi-User PDF ISBN: 978-1-62285-143-0

Printed in the United States of America

042013 Lake Book Manufacturing, Inc., Melrose Park, IL

10 9 8 7 6 5 4 3 2 1

To Our Readers:
We have done our best to make sure all Internet addresses in this book were active and appropriate when we went to press. However, the author and the Publisher have no control over, and assume no liability for, the material available on those Internet sites or on other Web sites they may link to. Any comments or suggestions can be sent by e-mail to comments@speedingstar.com or to the address below:

Speeding Star
Box 398, 40 Industrial Road
Berkeley Heights, NJ 07922
USA
www.speedingstar.com

Cover Illustration: Daryll Collins

Table of Contents

1

THE SMELLERD ZOMBIES

"Whooooooo! . . . Yesssssssss! Oooooooh, yeah!" Leo's friend Chad bounced on his butt in the back of the bus. He pumped his fists over his head. He whipped his frizzy hair around. "Adios, Rrrrrrrrotfield!" Chad rolled the *R* in Rotfield as if it were a Spanish word. A half-circle of sweat spread out from the neck of his yellow T-shirt. On its front, a smiley face was gushing blood from its mouth. The words across Chad's belly jiggled: "Zombies Make Me Smile."

Leo sat quietly next to his energetic friend. He relaxed against his stuffed backpack and closed his eyes. Leo felt this was the best way to scientifically observe his happiness. He could feel it ooze like warm honey from his chest.

Like most of Leo's warm-honey feelings, this one had to do with one thing: zombies. To Leo, *last day of school* meant *only three days until Smellerd Summer Camp.* And that meant finally solving the mystery of the Smellerd zombies.

❧

"Door!" Leo's mother called from outside as Leo ran into the kitchen after school. He pushed the door shut with the back of his heel.

"Backpack!" she called out. Leo slid off his backpack and hung it on the hook. He grabbed a banana and headed upstairs to get to work.

"Kiss!" Leo's mother yelled as he was halfway up the stairs. *Ugh.* Leo groaned but went and found his mother gardening in the backyard. He knew from experience he should just get it over with. That was the best way to deal with the fact that his mother still acted like he was one instead of eleven.

When he was finally alone in his room, Leo cracked open his laptop and logged onto his Zombie Zappers Web site.

He squinted at the familiar green screen. *For all your zombie needs*, it read across the top. Did that image of the waving zombie hand look like an octopus? Leo made a note to change it later. Right now he had to post an important update. He clicked on the "Z-News" link and started typing.

> *ZombieZapper #1 here with a special update on the mystery of the Smellerd zombies. What*

you are about to read is NOT a ghost story. This is FACT. I researched it myself.

- *Fact #1: In June 1981, Guppy Scout Troop 483 went on a fishing trip at Smellerd Summer Camp . . . and they never came back.*

- *Fact #2: The bodies of the twelve young boys were never found.*

- *Fact #3: Scientist Dr. Phineas Funkle devoted the last ten years of his life to this mystery. Sadly, few of his notes remain. In the last days of his life, Dr. F wrote:*

> I can scarcely believe I am writing these words. But I must. All of my research points to one conclusion. The evidence cannot be denied. Simply put, the Guppy Scouts have turned into zombies. But they are zombies of the most unusual nature. This situation requires the utmost care. I tremble even to write these words for fear they will be read by the wrong eyes.

Never fear, Dr. F! ZombieZapper #1 is on the case! Below are my three main points of investigation:

- *Question #1: What caused the Guppy Scouts to turn into zombies?*

- *Question #2: Where are the zombies now?*

- *Question #3: What makes the Smellerd zombies so "unusual"?*

More updates to come after I return from my undercover mission at Smellerd Summer Camp. Stay tuned!

P.S. Chad says to check out the merchandise section. He's featuring two new T-shirt designs. Twenty percent off for first-time buyers.

Leo read over his work. Satisfied, he clicked "Update Now." Hmmm. What next? Leo thought about getting an early start on packing. He knew he had tons of laundry to do first. He scanned his room. The laundry basket had completely disappeared under the pile of dirty clothes at the end of his bed. On second thought, what about *Zombies versus Aliens*? He was so close to making Level 10.

Leo had just flicked on his video console when he heard a familiar *swoosh* behind him. He spun around. "What are you doing out here?" he yelped.

2

PIECE OF MIND

"Roger, you're not supposed to come out here!" Leo jumped up and stood guarding his closed bedroom door. Who knew when his bossy stepsister Shelly would pop in. She was always up for a brainstorm about how to make Leo "cooler." Or his parents could get suddenly "interested" in Leo's zombie science "hobby." Now that summer was here, Leo was officially a sixth grader. Old enough in his opinion to be left alone, but his family didn't agree.

Roger was in sixth grade too. Or he would have been if he went to school. Instead, Roger lived in a secret lab behind the back wall of Leo's closet. The wall slid open with a *swoosh* at the press of a button.

Roger was a half-zombie. He was just a little green and (mostly) okay to smell. His family had been wiped out in a zombie attack four years ago. Roger had been licked during the attack but not fully bitten. His heart still beat at least twenty times a day. "And it still swells with emotion," he often said proudly in his fake British accent.

With sunglasses, a hat, and half a pack of Band-Aids, Roger could pass as human. But it was risky for Roger to go outside. Four years ago, Roger's ear had been blown off by the wind during a T-ball game. Luckily, Leo had been the only one to notice.

Leo didn't know anything about zombies back then. Still, he somehow knew not to be scared. He brought Roger home after the game and glued the ear back on. That was the day Roger and Leo broke ground on their secret lab.

Roger had spent the past four years living and working in the lab. Because Roger barely needed to sleep, he was the ideal lab partner. Roger had made more than his fair share of amazing zombie science discoveries. But sadly, he was still as far away as ever from finding a cure for his own half-zombiehood.

"Roger, let's go back in the lab," Leo hissed. "If Shelly sees you, she'll freak!"

"I don't care!" Roger said. And for once, he sounded like a regular American kid.

"Shhhhhhhh!" Leo hissed. "Roger, what's wrong with you? You're being—" Leo searched his brain for just the right Roger kind of word. *"Reckless."*

"Reckless, eh?" Roger said. "Like this?" And he reached his arm inside a hole in the back of his neck. He pulled out a handful of brains and flung them across the room. They landed like a clump of oatmeal on Leo's forehead.

"AAAAAaaaaaagh!" Leo screamed.

"Leo, honey? Are you okay?" His mom's voice called from downstairs.

"I'm fine!" he yelled. He opened the door a crack. "Just lost my guy in my game. Everything's cool."

"That's enough screen time," his mom yelled up.

"Okay, it's off," Leo called back before closing his door. He carefully wiped the brains off his face and into his cupped hand.

"As you can see, I came out here to give you a piece of my mind," Roger said. His

British accent was back, though his voice was way too calm. "That's what you're after anyway. Isn't that right, old chap?"

"I have no idea what you're talking about." Leo walked over to Roger. "Hold still." He carefully scooped the brains back into Roger's neck. Then he sealed the hole with a Band-Aid.

"I'm talking about your latest Zombie Zappers update," Roger said. "This is FACT. I researched it myself," Roger quoted in a singsong voice. "Yourself, indeed!" Roger let out a dignified huff. "I was the one who discovered Dr. Funkle's lost notes!"

"C'mon, Roger," Leo began. "You know I can't write about you on my site. If people find out about you, they'll put you in a zoo or a museum or at least juvenile detention—"

"My, my." For a kid who hadn't grown in four years, Roger suddenly looked awfully tall. "What a lousy excuse," he said. Then he stepped gracefully over a pile of smelly shoes in Leo's closet. He pressed the button behind Leo's blue bathrobe. Then he disappeared back into the lab with a *swoosh*.

3

WELCOME TO CAMP SMELLERD

Leo and Roger didn't talk at all the next day. It was the first day since they'd met that Leo hadn't seen Roger's greenish face. That was just fine with Leo. Even looking at his closet door made Leo mad.

The following day, Sunday, was packing day. Leo tried to avoid Roger as he looked for stray socks and his new swimming trunks. He had to go into the lab to find his notebook. Roger didn't even look up when he heard the *swoosh*. In fact, he shifted his body and turned his laptop away from Leo.

What was that about? Obviously Roger was up to something. Leo was dying to know what it was. He started digging through a box behind Roger. Crouching, he caught a glimpse of Roger's screen. It was a picture of some dumb duck. The bird was dead. Its body was floating on green, scummy water. Leo squinted to read the words under the picture. "The death of Lake Moan began in 1981, just a few short days after—"

"Hey!" Roger snapped the laptop shut. "This is private." Then he glared at Leo, who pretended he had just found the pair of rubber gloves he'd been looking for. Leo shoved the gloves in his pocket and left the lab with a huff and a *swoosh*.

Chad and Leo had signed up for camp together. The first week of camp was Nature Week. That meant they'd spend their days cleaning up litter, learning about conservation, and doing other activities around the woods. Chad had wanted to hold out for Arts Week. But Leo had talked him into the earlier slot. "We don't want too many distractions," Leo had argued. "As it is, we'll have to pretend to do chores while we look for the zombies."

That Monday morning, Chad and his cousin Anita arrived to pick up Leo for the three-hour ride. Anita had turned sixteen in January. She was going to be working at Camp Smellerd as a counselor this summer.

"Be good," Leo's mom said as she hugged him good-bye on the sidewalk outside the car.

"Got everything?" Leo's dad asked. "Sunscreen, bug spray, flashlight, toothpaste, vitamins?"

"Yes, *yes*," Leo said. Were his parents having a who-can-embarrass-Leo-the-most contest?

Leo slid into the backseat and slammed the door. "Okay, see ya! Bye! So long!"

"Bye, pumpkin!" his mother yelled. Leo settled back in his seat, but not before he caught a glimpse of something—someone— greenish looking out at him from his bedroom window. *Roger!* Roger's mouth was open. He looked like he wanted to say something.

Leo shook his head at Roger. "What are you doing?" he mouthed. As the car rolled past the house, Leo pointed with his head for Roger to get back in the lab.

But Roger didn't move. He reached for something. The sign flashed in the window. It read, "WAIT FOR ME."

<hr />

"Leo? Leo? Earth to Leo!" Anita was waving to Leo in the rearview mirror as they whizzed along the highway.

"Huh?" Leo smiled weakly. He shook his head, trying to shake away the worry Roger's sign had planted there. What did Roger mean, anyway? Wait for him where? Why? For how long? What did it mean to wait for your secret half-zombie friend who could never leave his hidden laboratory? *What did Roger know?*

"You look like you've just seen a ghost!" Anita's dazzling smile brought Leo back to reality. Leo was glad he was in the backseat. He wouldn't have wanted to sit next to Anita. It was like sitting too close to the screen in a movie theater. He got dizzy.

"Anyway, Leo, as I was saying, I am just so incredibly thrilled to be a part of the Smellerd team," Anita said. "What an opportunity this is for me. I'm really looking forward to growing through the experience, you know?"

Leo nodded. Anita brushed back her long, coffee-colored hair. Then she brushed back her white feather earrings that dangled past her shoulders. Leo loved how Anita talked. She was so thoughtful and confident. She sounded like somebody running for president.

"Leo? You still there?" Anita laughed. In the mirror, her brown eyes focused on him for a second.

"Ummm. Yeah? I'm just, you know," Leo said. *Ugh.* He definitely wasn't running for president anytime soon.

After a while, the car turned off the smooth road onto bumpy gravel. They passed a faded wooden sign. It showed a chipmunk in a striped vest and the words, "Welcome to Camp Smellerd!" The car crunched along slowly to the main cabin. The blazing summer sun gave way to shade squirming beneath tall oaks.

"Here comes the hard part," Anita said. The road curved to the right. Then a sharp, sour smell hit Leo in the face. It made him cough into his hand.

"Zombies?" he mouthed to Chad, who had already turned around to make a *Z* in the air with his finger.

"Um, can we stop?" Leo managed to say, but Anita was already pulling over. The gang piled out of the car.

"It's such a tragedy," Anita continued as if she were in the middle of a conversation with someone else. "Since before we were born." Anita wistfully swept a hand in front of her as if to point out something. "Can you believe it?"

Leo tried to memorize what was in front of him so he could find this place later. He saw the usual trees, then grass, then sand, then rocks, then—

"Is that moss?" Chad asked. He walked toward what looked like a light green field. "No, wait a minute, it's *moving*."

"There's something under the ground!" Leo shouted, and he and Chad charged toward it.

But a second later they stopped just as fast. "Oooooooooh," Chad said loudly, while Leo cringed. *Stupid mistake #1,* he thought. They had clearly arrived at some kind of water's edge. The stinky green stuff was just algae floating on the surface.

Leo turned to see if Anita was watching, but she was still in her own world. She was squatting in the sand, peering into the water.

"This is Lake Moan," she said when she saw Leo looking at her.

Lake Moan. The lake from Roger's laptop, Leo thought.

"As you can see, it has a bad case of algal bloom, or green tide," Anita continued. "The algae grow out of control. It has completely destroyed the lake's ecosystem. No other life can survive here."

That explained the dead duck in Roger's picture, and the green water. But why was Roger—

"Don't touch it!" Anita shrieked suddenly. And Leo turned to see Chad pull his hand sharply away from the water's surface.

"The algae cover might still be polluted," Anita explained. "You need special gloves to handle it." After a pause, Anita continued, "At least, that's my theory. You see, the algal bloom began on June 20, 1981. That was just one week after the radioactive blast at Brainland's nuclear power plant. I know what you're thinking." Anita held out a hand in front of her as if to stop the objection that was forming in Leo's mouth.

"I know, I know, we're 200 miles from Brainland. That's why cleanup crews never came this far out. They said the damage had been 'contained.' But this lake is *directly* downstream from the Brainland plant. The algae covered Lake Moan so incredibly fast. I'm convinced the blast of 1981 caused this environmental catastrophe. Of course, that was a long time ago. There's no danger now as long as you're wearing the proper gear."

Hands on hips, Anita squinted out at the lake. The sun reflected off the slimy algae and onto her face. It made her skin look slightly green. *Like Roger,* Leo thought.

"I plan to clean up this lake tomorrow." Anita turned to Chad and Leo. Her eyes looked both sad and determined. "Are you guys with me?"

"Uhhhhhh," Chad began. He twisted the tip of his shoe in the sand.

"Yes," Leo said, punching Chad in the arm. Leo looked straight into Anita's face. "Yes, we are." If Roger was researching this lake, chances are it had something to do with the Smellerd zombies. Tomorrow they would look for clues. *Sorry, Roger,* Leo thought. There was no way to wait for him, whatever that meant. Disappointing Anita was out of the question.

4

LAKE MOAN

That night during Campfire Chat, Anita gave a speech about Lake Moan. Leo had never seen sixth graders sit so still before. Afterward, campers ages eleven and older got a chance to sign up for Anita's cleanup crew. Chad and Leo had already taken the first two spots. Anita had enough supplies for just eighteen more helpers. So kids pushed and elbowed their way to the sign-up sheet.

The next day, Chad and Leo showed up at Lake Moan right after breakfast. Leo had his zombie field notebook with him, as well as two extra pens.

"Let's not get separated," Leo whispered to Chad. Last night before lights out, Leo had told Chad about Roger's research and his weird sign in the window.

"Officially on high alert," Chad said, karate chopping an invisible zombie with his hand.

That made the tight feeling in Leo's stomach relax a little. Chad may have been joking, but he was still the best zombie fighter Leo knew.

⚬ ⚬ ◆ ⚬ ⚬

"Safety is number one," Anita was saying as Leo and Chad joined the circle of eager middle schoolers surrounding her. "Please take one of each and suit up." Anita pointed to four neat stacks of white, crinkly clothing: booties, pants, jackets, gloves, and hoods that snapped right under the chin. "These items will protect your skin from any pollutants."

"But there's no place to change," said one girl with a frizzy blonde ponytail. She looked anxiously down at the white pants balled up in her hands. She was clearly more nervous about changing in public than getting soaked in polluted algae.

"Put them on right over your clothes," Anita said. She smiled kindly at the girl, who smiled weakly back at her. "See? I'm doing it too." And Anita tugged on her own safety suit as well.

Then Anita went around and helped her crew adjust their buckles and straps. Some kids giggled as they snapped on their white hoods.

"I can't hear," one girl with blue braces whined.

"I'm too hot," said an eighth grade boy with a fuzzy upper lip.

Ten minutes later, the group of ragtag kids in mismatched socks and stained T-shirts had been transformed. In their sparkling white suits, they looked like algae-fighting superheroes.

"You look wonderful!" Anita said, clapping her hands together. Next she passed out safety goggles. Then came supplies: brushes, nets with long handles, and rags. As Leo reached for his supplies, Anita stopped him. "I need you and Chad in the boat with me," she said. She pointed at a steel canoe near the water's edge. "You can paddle while I operate the skimmer."

Sitting in the middle of the canoe was a machine that looked like a funky vacuum cleaner. Leo and Chad inspected the long, bendy hose that snaked out from a giant orange tank.

Meanwhile, Anita was dividing the crew into groups. One group would scrub the dock.

Another would wipe off the rocks along the water's edge. The tallest kids would wade into the water and push the algae toward the middle with the nets.

"I'll be there with Chad and Leo in the boat," Anita said. "We'll suck up the algae into the skimmer. Ready, everyone? Let's get to work!"

Leo had planned to use his awesome powers of observation to find zombie clues. But he barely had a chance to glance around before the panic began.

Looking back, Leo couldn't say exactly when or how it started. At first, things went as expected. There were some "eeeeews" and "yucks" as the kids sank their gloved hands into the green scum. The eighth grader with the fuzzy lip scooped up a clump of green goo and flung it at a friend. Anita kicked him out for that and sent him to clean the latrines.

It was actually kind of peaceful in the boat. Leo liked pushing his oar through the muck, even though clumps of it splashed up and stuck to his white suit from time to time. Chad was in a good mood too. He hummed to himself as he expertly steered from the back.

"Here's good," Anita said, and they stopped in the middle of the lake. Then Anita placed the skimmer's hose gently on the water's surface. She flicked on the switch, and a pleasant whooshing sound filled the air.

Little by little, the lake cleared. Black water started to show around the edges. Then the ring of clean water slowly got wider and wider.

Chad was the one who heard it first. "What's that noise?" he asked, peering out across the lake. Leo listened. There was still the *whoosh* of the skimmer. But there was a new sound as well. It was a gurgling noise coming from under the water. Leo sat up. The noise grew louder and louder until—

"*AAAAAAAAAAAAHHHHHHHHHHHHH HHHHHHHH.*" From the lake's shore came a long, low moan.

After that, the screams of the cleanup crew drowned out any other noises. Then there were kids splashing everywhere. Brushes and nets went flying. Kids were running away in all directions. They were screaming streaks of white shooting through the woods.

"Stay calm," Anita said. And for a second, the lake did seem calm again. Brushes and nets bobbed on the water's surface. The skimmer whooshed. The ring of clean black water continued to widen.

"What's that?" Chad pointed at the clean water by the shore. Something silvery flashed to the surface. Then came another flash, and another. Water bubbled around the flashes. Then, in each spot, a silver dome started to rise.

CHAPTER

5

SOMETHING IN THE WATER

L eo's heart was pounding out of his chest even before his brain figured out what he was looking at. Each dome was covered in tiny scales. And each dome had a face: glowing white eyes and a gaping black mouth. On each side, a row of flaps—gill slits—slowly opened and closed.

They were fish. Giant, gurgling fish rising out of the water.

"Mmmmmmmmhhhh," a fish moaned. Green slime oozed out of gashes on the back of its head. The slime gushed down its back and pooled on the surface of the water.

"Hhhhhhhnnnnnn." Another fish turned up its head to the sun and moaned like a wolf howling at the moon. "Aaaaaannnnngh," it wailed again. And then two human hands—rotting, kid-sized hands—rose out of the water. They grabbed the fish head on both sides as it barfed green slime onto its own face. And now Chad was screaming, "Zombies! Zombies!"

A dozen of them broke the surface. Each one had a wet scarf tied around its fleshy neck. Each one was wearing a ragged vest, a belt, and shorts. Green, gashed arms and legs shot out from the uniforms.

"The Guppy Scouts . . ." Leo gasped.

". . . are fish-headed zombies!" Chad yelped.

"They're coming toward us!" Anita hissed. She twisted frantically in the boat. "We're surrounded!"

Moaning and gurgling, the fish-headed zombies turned toward the canoe. Their dead eyes seemed to look right at Chad, Leo, and Anita. Leo could hear mud sucking at the zombies' feet as they lurched forward. They swayed with every step, sending ripples over the dark water. The ripples lapped at the edge of the boat. It rocked back and forth, back and forth.

With each gentle motion, fear sloshed inside Leo's body. The sick feeling washed over his chest and stomach. It spilled into his arms and legs. *Think, think!* Leo shouted at his own brain. But his brain just whirred like the skimmer in the boat.

And still the zombies closed in. They held their arms out straight in front of them, blackened fingers dangling. Then Chad was shaking Leo, trying to tell him something.

"Their hands are webbed." Chad pointed at the green folds of skin that stretched between the rotten fingers. "Their feet probably are too. That means we can't outswim them. We'll have to escape by boat."

Leo gulped. "Here." He handed his oar to Anita. "Use it as a weapon. Whatever happens to us, protect yourself." Chad nodded in agreement.

"But—" Anita began as her fingers closed around the handle.

"I'll manage," said Leo.

Chad's eyes scanned the water, then stopped. He paddled the canoe toward a net floating about twenty feet away. He leaned over the side of the canoe and grabbed the net's handle with his free hand. "It's better than nothing. Make it work, Leo," he said. "I'll row from the back. All you have to do is fend them off so we can get the boat to shore. We'll have a better chance of escaping on land."

Anita and Leo balanced themselves on either side of the canoe. Chad settled into position at the back. He looked for the best escape route. "Fewer zombies this way," he said, pointing to his left. "Let's go!"

CHAPTER

6

TAKE ME
TO YOUR LEADER

Chad's muscles must have been in overdrive from all the excitement. It was amazing how fast the boat glided over the water. Chad yelled with every stroke: "Go! Go! Go! Go! Go!"

For one glorious second, it seemed as if they were going to make it to shore. No zombies lay in the path of water ahead. As they picked up speed, the water formed a neat V behind the boat. A fine spray of algae slime coated their faces.

"Whoooo-hooooo!" Chad yelled, laughing now. "The Chad is too fast for fishies. Smell ya later, tuna-heads!" And even Leo was able to smile a little. But Anita stayed poised on her knees, oar raised.

"Stay down," she hissed. "Focus on your tasks!" She wiped the slime out of her eyes with two gloved fingers.

"Go! Go! Go!" Chad yelled. And the boat did go. But instead of gliding forward, it was slowly tipping upward. Anita screamed as the she slid toward the back of the boat.

"One of them is under us!" Chad yelled.

In his right hand, Leo gripped the handle of his net like a sword. With his free hand, he pulled himself up to the edge of the boat. He pushed the top half of his body over the side with a grunt. Sure enough, a silver-domed head was pressing up against the canoe's bow. Its lips were suctioned against the boat's bottom. Its zombie hands gripped either side.

This zombie was bigger than the others. And it wasn't wearing a scarf and vest. A torn plaid shirt and jeans covered the human part of its body.

The troop leader! Leo thought.

"Attack!" Chad yelled.

Leo closed his eyes and lunged. He felt the end of his net make contact. Then he felt it sink into soft flesh and pop out the other side.

"Bllaaaaaap," the zombie gurgled. The boat smacked back down on the water.

Leo opened his eyes. The zombie troop leader's fish head rose in front of the canoe. Leo's white plastic net stuck out from either side of its neck. The fish head squirmed. Its white eyes rolled in their sockets. Its mouth opened and closed as if it were screaming, but only gurgling sounds came out.

Chad started to row, but the boat just bumped into the zombie's plaid belly. Chad didn't know how to steer around it. Its green arms were waving wildly in all directions. Finally, one of its hands brushed against the plastic net handle. It gripped. *Sluuuurp.* It pulled the net right out of its neck.

"Reverse!" Chad yelled, paddling frantically. Anita rowed with the other oar, while Leo plunged his hands into the water to help. Leo felt the silky water slide over his arms as he made one backward circle, then another. He cupped his hands and pushed them through the waves—until his fingers brushed against the edge of something soft. Suddenly, he felt a webbed hand grip his wrist.

"Noooooo!" Leo roared. He jerked his arm so hard his whole body fell backward into the boat. And he had brought something with him. Hanging from his own, living arm was the severed arm of the zombie, still gripping his wrist. Its bloody stump dripped onto Leo's lap.

"Uhhhh." Leo held back a gag as he uncurled the zombie fingers from his wrist and the arm dropped into his lap.

"No!" Chad was screaming. Leo turned around. Chad and Anita had both lost their oars. Chad was on his belly, head over the stern of the boat. Chad stared open-mouthed at the water underneath his face. To Leo's left, Anita was sitting completely still. Her hands were folded neatly in her lap. Her eyes were closed, and she was whispering to herself.

"Chad? Anita?" Leo said. He wanted to add, "Don't give up," but he didn't get the chance.

The other zombies had already caught up with the boat. Their green hands gripped the top of the canoe from all sides. The canoe started rocking wildly. Leo grabbed the ripped-off zombie arm with both hands. He smacked the green hands with the rotting arm, as if he were playing zombie Whac-A-Mole. But the fingers only gripped the edge of the boat tighter.

FACING UNDEATH

"That's when I lost it," Anita would later say. "I admit it. I broke down and cried like a baby."

"I almost peed my pants!" Chad said. "I thought, 'This is it. The moment of zombification.'"

And Leo? Looking back, Leo remembered fear. Oh yes. Fear like a cage around him. But he also remembered something breaking through that fear. A cool, sweet ray of hope. For at that moment, he saw a kid slowly riding a bike toward the lakeshore.

The kid was wearing Leo's old orange sneakers from second grade. His jeans were two sizes too big. And his T-shirt draped down to his knees. It had "Zombies Have More Fun" written in Chad's handwriting across the front. A huge straw hat topped off the kid's outfit— Leo's mother's gardening hat. And under the brim was the unmistakably greenish face of Roger. "Your zombie in shining armor," Roger would later joke.

Sitting in that boat, defending his life with a zombie arm stump, Leo couldn't laugh. But he'd laugh plenty later, remembering. Because Roger looked like a panicked tree sloth. He was moving as fast as he could in his own half-zombie way.

Roger's bike fell sideways to the ground. He stood up and stomped into the water. "I'm coming! I'm coming!" he yelled over and over again, as if they couldn't tell. "Oh dear, oh dear me," he said as he waded deeper. Then Roger dove underwater and swam toward them. His head popped up behind the fray of zombies clawing at the canoe.

By now, one of the zombies had the upper half of its body tilted inside the boat. Its hands were wrapped around one of Anita's feet, while its legs shot into the sky.

Splaaatuuunk. Another zombie flopped into the boat. Leo felt its hands grip him around the knee.

"Oh dear," Roger said another time. "Here goes." Then Roger grabbed one of the fish heads from behind. He held the head on either side, lifted it slightly out of the water, and spun the zombie around to face him.

"Aaaaaaaaargh," the zombie moaned. It opened its giant, dripping mouth. In an act of sheer bravery or utter foolishness, Roger stuck his arm inside. The group held their breath. But the fatal bite never came. Instead, the zombie contentedly sucked on Roger's elbow joint. "Ooooooooooooh." All the air inside Roger seemed to seep out in one long, relieved sigh.

"Roger?" Leo looked at Roger making his way through the fish-headed zombies as calmly as if he were walking through a crowded mall. Then Leo turned his attention back to the zombie that had latched onto his leg. Something was wrong. Not bad wrong. Good wrong. Zombies-aren't-eating-my-flesh wrong.

"Help me up," Roger said when he reached the canoe. He held out his hand, and Leo easily pulled Roger's slight body into the boat. "Excuse me," Roger said to the fish-headed zombie who was now nibbling on the cuff of Leo's white pants. Roger stepped over the zombie's silver head and sat down on the bench next to Leo. Then he leaned over and hugged

Leo around the neck. "Dear me," Roger said. "I'm afraid I'm quite overcome."

"Hey, Roger?" Chad said. He was trying to push off a zombie who was licking a green spot off the back of his jacket. "What's going on?"

"I am so very relieved that you are okay." Roger smiled sweetly at the crew in the boat. "Why, hello there. I'm Roger, half-zombie." Roger held out his hand to Anita, who was shaking with laughter.

"It's s-so t-t-t-ticklish!" she squealed. One of the zombies was chewing at the edge of her hood.

"Um, Roger? That's really great, man, but I meant, um, what's going on with these zombies?" Chad said.

"Oh, yes of course," Roger said. "Well, as I suspected, they're filter feeders."

"Huh?" Chad looked to Leo for an explanation.

Leo looked closer at the zombie nibbling at his cuff. He realized the zombie wasn't nibbling after all. It was sucking on the cloth and twisting it in its mouth. Like the way Chad sucked on the paper that came off a cupcake.

"They don't have teeth!" Leo said.

"They don't need them," Roger explained.

"That must be b-b-b-because . . . HAAAAAHAAAAA! HA-hooo-hoooo!" Anita managed to push off her zombie for a second. "Because they eat the algae! They're sucking the algae off our clothes, and my h-h-h-hair!" Anita squeaked. The zombie nibbled at the end of Anita's ponytail, which had freed itself from her hood during the battle.

"Exactly." Roger smiled. "No chewing required."

"Oh, poor things," Anita said. She patted her zombie's fish head affectionately. "We took away your food source, didn't we?" Then she slid over to the skimmer. It was still humming quietly on the middle bench. She dropped the skimmer's hose over the edge of the boat.

"Auntie Anita is going to take care of everything," she said. Then she bent down and flicked the skimmer's switch. Green goop gushed out of the hose and back onto the lake's surface.

Plop! Plunk! Splash! One by one, the zombies dove back into the water. A green circle began to spread slowly outward from the boat. And soon the gurgling sounds of happy fish-headed zombies filled the warm summer air.

8

ZOMBIE SCIENCE
TO THE RESCUE

"It's days like these I'm glad I'm not a vampire," Roger said. He pulled off his hat and lifted his head toward the sun as the canoe drifted with the breeze. "Mmmmmm. What a perfect summer day," he said, "and for zombie science as well."

"No doubt," Leo agreed, stretching out on his seat.

"And for Lake Moan as well," Anita added. Arms crossed, she looked out on the algae-covered water with a satisfied smile.

"Uhhhhh." Chad looked around at his smiling friends. "Am I the only one with questions? Like, uhhh, *What in the world are you doing here, Roger?*"

"I suppose the situation does require some explanation." Roger placed his hat carefully back on his head. "Well, if I could have come sooner, I would have. But I'm afraid I've never been a terribly fast bike rider, even when I was fully living.

"You see, I've been riding my bike for the past twenty hours at least. I took off right after you drove away." He nodded politely at Anita. "I was so very mad at you, Leo. I was convinced you were taking credit for my work."

"I didn't mean to, Roger," Leo said. "I'm really sorry."

"But now I see that I just felt left out," Roger continued. "And perhaps a bit jealous. So I did a wrong much worse than yours, Leo. You see, I knew a great deal about the Smellerd zombies, and I didn't tell you. Then, as you were leaving, I realized my horrible mistake. You needed my valuable information."

"Like, say, the zombies have fish heads?" Chad said. "Yeah, that would have been good to know."

"And that they eat algae," Anita added.

"And that they're totally harmless!" Leo laughed.

"Oh, but I wasn't entirely sure on that point, you see," Roger said. "I could not be one hundred percent sure of your safety. And so, I came to warn you."

"But Roger, how did you know all this?" Chad asked.

"Well, it was a simple matter of research, logic, and a hunch," Roger began. He twisted a Band-Aid on his wrist and his hand fell off.

"Excuse me," he said, reaffixing it with a fresh Band-Aid from his pocket.

"As I was saying, it all began with research," he continued. "The radioactive blast at Brainland's nuclear power plant has long been a topic of interest to me."

"Me too!" Anita said.

"As is Lake Moan's algal bloom." Roger smiled shyly at Anita. "And you sparked my interest in the Smellerd zombies, Leo," Roger continued. "Was it just a coincidence that all three of these important events happened in June of 1981? I think not!" Roger dramatically waved one finger in the air. "That's where logic came in. Here, your help was key, Leo. Remember the three questions you posted on the Web site? One: What caused the Guppy Scouts to turn into zombies? Two: Where were they? And three: What made them so unusual?"

Leo nodded.

"Well, I couldn't get those out of my head. I started with question one—the cause. What made sense? I knew radiation could change the life cycles of living things. I also knew the Guppy Scouts were fishing on Lake Moan shortly after the radioactive blast. Could the blast have turned them into zombies? That seemed like a very reasonable guess to me.

"Next question: Where were they? Where, indeed. I knew the zombies couldn't have gone far. There was no trace of them, no reports of sightings. The zombies had to be at camp. But where could they hide unnoticed? Where was the one place campers never went?"

"Lake Moan!" Anita answered.

"Exactly," Roger said. "That prompted another question: How come these zombies stayed in the lake? How come they didn't come out to feast on humans like proper zombies? They must be feasting on something else, I thought. What else could that be? The answer was clear. They were feasting on the only available food source—the algae, as we now know.

"After that came my hunch. Dr. Funkle had called the zombies 'unusual.' Why? Well, that's when I remembered one of the most basic principles of biology—"

"Adaptation!" Leo yelled. He shot to his feet, sending the canoe rocking.

"M'boy!" Roger said. He held out his hand and carefully high-fived Leo.

"The zombies didn't have fish heads right away!" Leo said. He was panting a little from the excitement of what he knew. "Their bodies changed to meet the needs of their environment. I mean, this usually takes thousands of years. But under radioactive conditions, it happened much, much faster.

Their human heads changed to fish heads! Fish heads are simply better for eating the algae at Lake Moan—"

"That explains the webbed hands too!" Chad added. "The zombies' hands changed so they could swim faster around the lake!"

"And so, my friends," Roger began. His face was serious now. "You can see that these zombies are the most exquisite of creatures. The first of their kind. Perfectly suited to their unique habitat. Both frightening and fascinating. We can understand why Dr. Funkle wanted to protect them. In the wrong hands, the zombies could be caged—or worse."

"But nobody will ever find them," Anita said, "right?" She looked from Chad to Leo to Roger with fierce eyes. "Promise." She stuck out her arm and spread her fingers. Leo put his white hand on hers. Then came Chad's tan one. Roger's greenish hand completed the stack.

"I promise to protect the secret of the Smellerd fish-headed zombies," Anita said.

"I promise to protect the secret of the Smellerd fish-headed zombies," the boys repeated.

And as they pulled back their hands, they heard the sound of trampling feet coming from the woods. Then came voices and barking dogs. Police in blue uniforms ran onto the shore.

"Evacuate the lake," a voice boomed over a megaphone. "I repeat, remove your boat from the lake. You are in grave danger."

Leo looked out across the water. The lake was once again completely green. Then he looked at his brave friends. Anita sat up straight. Her face was perfectly calm as she watched the officials on shore. Roger was pulling at the brim of his hat. Chad's eyes were wide. His mouth was squirming as if he was about to crack up. Then Leo felt his own laughter rising into his throat like a balloon about to pop.

"We'd better go talk to them," he squeaked.

Chad leaned over the edge of the canoe and fished out the oars floating on the surface. "I'll row," he said. With each stroke, beautiful green swirls spread outward from the boat. It glided without a bump all the way to the shore.

EPILOGUE

"Everyone knows there's no such thing as zombies," Anita told the police officers. "And fish-headed zombies?" Anita laughed her silvery laugh. "I'm afraid someone's been listening to too many ghost stories." By the time Anita was done, the police officers were apologizing to her for the inconvenience.

Later, Anita explained to camp leaders that she had uncovered new information about the algae on Lake Moan. "It's actually very important to the lake's food web," she told them. Six months later, they made Lake Moan a protected nature preserve. Nobody would bother the zombies ever again.

That afternoon, Anita drove Roger back to the lab. He spent the whole ride telling her his own story of half-zombiehood. Roger had never been happier to see his messy home.

"Did you see how those police dogs were all sniffing me?" Roger said. And he plopped down in front of his laptop with a happy sigh. When Anita left, she promised to come back and visit often. And she really did.

Chad and Leo finished Nature Week by clearing brush along the hiking trails. That summer, Chad figured out how to draw an awesome mosquito. Leo added ten new species to his list of "Unusual Plants I Have Seen."

As for his Web site, Leo never did post another update about the Smellerd zombies. Roger did. He made the whole thing up. His story included a bike chase, a rotting tuna fish sandwich, a cowboy hat, and four best friends.

Read each title in **ZOMBIE ZAPPERS**

ZOMBIE CAMP
ZOMBIE ZAPPERS BOOK 1

Get to know Zombie Zappers Leo, Chad, and the rest of the gang as they try to solve the mystery of the Smellerd zombies at summer camp. What nightmarish surprise will they find waiting for them at Lake Moan?

ISBN: 978-1-62285-003-7

ZOMBIE FIELD DAY
ZOMBIE ZAPPERS BOOK 2

Join the Zombie Zappers back at school for the next round of zombie mayhem. When Rotfield Middle School students start turning into zombies, Leo and his friends are the only ones who might be able to save them. Can they discover the cause of this outbreak before it's too late?

ISBN: 978-1-62285-005-1

THE ZOMBIE NEXT DOOR
ZOMBIE ZAPPERS BOOK 3

What if your next-door neighbor were a zombie? The Zombie Zappers return to find out exactly why Leo's neighbor is acting so strange in this suspenseful book. Leo learns a valuable lesson in the process.

ISBN: 978-1-62285-010-5

DOWN, ZOMBIE, DOWN!
ZOMBIE ZAPPERS BOOK 4

The Zombie Zappers jump back into action when a unique zombie outbreak spreads to their hometown. Leo will have to join forces with Chad's new best friend if they want to stop Rotfield from being overrun by a new breed of zombie.

ISBN: 978-1-62285-015-0